E
Rey

MARGRET & H.A. REY'S
Curious George
Goes to a Movie

Illustrated in the style of H. A. Rey by Vipah Interactive

Houghton Mifflin Company   Boston 1998

Copyright © 1998 by Houghton Mifflin Company

Based on the character of Curious George®, created by Margret and H. A. Rey.
Illustrated by Vipah Interactive: C. Becker, D. Fakkel, M. Jensen, S. SanGiacomo, C. Yu.

The text of this book is set in 17-pt. Adobe Garamond.
The illustrations are watercolor and charcoal pencil, reproduced in full color.

Library of Congress Cataloging-in-Publication Data

Curious George goes to a movie / based on the original character by Margret and H. A. Rey.
p. cm.
Summary: When his curiosity leads him to investigate how the movie gets onto the screen,
George, an inquisitive monkey, disrupts the show.
RNF ISBN 0-395-91901-0 PAP ISBN 0-395-91906-1 PABRD ISBN 0-395-92335-2
[1. Monkeys—Fiction. 2. Motion picture theatres—Fiction.]   I. Rey, Margret, 1906–1996.
II. Rey, H. A. (Hans Augusto), 1898–1977.
PZ7.C92163 1998
[E]—dc21   98-12370
                                                 CIP AC

Manufactured in the United States of America
WOZ 10 9 8 7 6 5 4 3 2 1

This is George.

George was a good little monkey and always very curious.

One afternoon George took a trip into town with his friend, the man with the yellow hat.

"Look, George," the man said as they walked by the theater. "The movie we've been waiting to see is here. If we hurry, we can make the next show."

"Two tickets, please," said the man with the yellow hat.

As they walked through the lobby, the smell of popcorn made George hungry. But when he stopped in front of the concession stand, his friend said, "Let's find our seats first, George. The movie is about to begin."

Inside the theater, they found two seats right in front. The man with the yellow hat whispered, "George, I'll go get some popcorn now. Stay here and watch the movie and please stay out of trouble."

George promised to be good.

George was enjoying the movie when all of a sudden a big dinosaur jumped onto the screen. It made George jump right out of his seat!

George was curious. Was he the only one to jump out of his seat? He looked around.

He was.

Looking around,
George saw a bright
light coming from a little
window at the back of the
theater. Was that what made
the movie appear on the screen?

9

Though he had promised to be good, little monkeys sometimes forget...

and soon George was at the back of the theater. But the window was so high, not even a monkey could climb up to see through it.

Usually there is a room behind a window, thought George. But how could he get inside?

Then he saw a door.

George raced up the stairs and peeked inside.

He saw a strange machine with two spinning wheels.

It was making a funny noise—and it was making the light that came through the window! Now he could see how the movie worked. But when he stepped into the room,

George was surprised to see a boy sitting in a chair. The boy was surprised to see a monkey standing in his room. In fact, the boy was so surprised, he jumped right out of his seat — and knocked the wheels right off the machine!

Downstairs in the theater, the audience began to shout and stomp their feet. They wanted to watch the movie...

but the movie was all over George!

George felt awful. The movie had stopped and it was all his fault.

"This is no place for a monkey," the boy said, working quickly to unwind George and rewind the movie. "Why don't you wait by that window while I fix this mess."

As George waited, he
looked out the window at the
audience and the big blank screen.
When he moved in front of the light that was coming
from the machine, he saw his shadow down below.
This reminded George of a trick!

He arranged his hands just so . . .

and a bunny appeared on the screen.

Then George made
a dog.

And a
duck.

And another
dog.

"It's a puppy!" someone from the audience shouted.

Others joined in. "It's a bird!" they said. George made the bird fly away.

Then the audience saw George's shadow up on the screen. They were delighted.

"It's a monkey!" a child yelled, and the audience laughed and clapped.

"This is better than a movie!" said a girl to her friend.

Just as George was about to run out of tricks, the boy announced that the movie was ready to go. The audience cheered — once for the movie and once for George!

The audience was still cheering when the man with the yellow hat ran into the room. "I thought I'd find you here, George," he said, and he apologized to the boy for the trouble George caused.

"He did give me a scare," the boy said. "But thanks to his hand

shadows, everyone waited patiently for the movie to be fixed."

Then the boy restarted the movie. "Would you like a treat for your performance, George?" he asked.

And before the dinosaur appeared again on the screen . . .

George and the man with the yellow hat were back in their seats.

This time, with popcorn.